JEKYLL
AND
LITTLE MISS
HYDE

Titles in Dark Reads:

Blood Moon
Barbara Catchpole

Doctor Jekyll and Little Miss Hyde
Tony Lee

Red Handed
Ann Evans

Ringtone
Tommy Donbavand

Ship of the Dead
Alex Woolf

Straw Men
Ann Evans

The Black-Eyed Girl
Tim Collins

The Girl in the Wall
Tommy Donbavand

Badger Publishing Limited, Oldmedow Road, Hardwick Industrial Estate, King's Lynn PE30 4JJ
Telephone: 01438 791037

www.badgerlearning.co.uk

DOCTOR JEKYLL AND LITTLE MISS HYDE

TONY LEE

Badger LEARNING

Doctor Jekyll and little Miss Hyde ISBN 978-1-78464-093-4

Publisher: Susan Ross
Senior Editor: Danny Pearson
Publishing Assistant: Claire Morgan
Copyeditor: Cheryl Lanyon
Designer: Bigtop Design Ltd
Illustrator: Emmanuel Cersier

2 4 6 8 10 9 7 5 3 1

Printed by Bell and Bain Ltd, Glasgow

CHAPTER 1

DOCTOR JEKYLL

She was the girl who always lost her seat in class, was picked last in games.

She was the girl who had her lunch stolen, and who had never kissed a boy.

But all of that was about to change...

Edwina Hyde was picked on by the school
bullies, Trina Ross and her 'Mean Girls' gang
of Mandy, Sandy and Candy.

Trina was the Queen of Rosedale High, and
if she didn't like you – your life was hell.

And Trina didn't like Edwina.

She would pinch Edwina's glasses – poor
Edwina was half-blind without them.
The gang of girls would laugh.

Edwina spent her break times in the science lab, helping the chemistry teacher, Doctor Jekyll. He was the strangest, most secretive man in the school.

He was always experimenting, but Edwina never knew what he was working on – until that fateful Wednesday.

As she entered, she saw Doctor Jekyll speaking into his phone.

"Batch seventeen works," he said. "I've created a drug that will make a person more self-confident."

"But I can't tell the school, or they'll know I've spent their money on my experiments!"

CHAPTER 2
GUINEA PIG

Edwina burst into the room.

"Let me try it!" she cried.

"I can't!" Doctor Jekyll replied. "It's not been tested on humans!"

"I'll be the guinea pig," Edwina continued. "And if you don't let me, I'll tell the school about your experiments!"

Doctor Jekyll knew he had no choice.

Edwina drank the potion – and the results were immediate!

Her spots cleared up, her teeth became straight, and her hair became shiny!

She felt cleverer and more powerful – and Edwina knew that she was beautiful!

But as pretty as she was now, her mind was much darker.

She was bitter, evil, and she picked on people worse than Trina ever did.

In fact, she even convinced Mandy, Sandy and Candy to join her, kicking Trina out of the gang!

This meant war!

CHAPTER 3
ANTIDOTE

Doctor Jekyll realised that something was wrong with the drug, but Edwina wouldn't listen.

He begged her to take an antidote, to return to normal – but she didn't want that!

And to stop him, she told terrible lies about him.

He was fired from the school!

Trina, seeing the science teacher escorted from the building, realised the truth. That Doctor Jekyll had created this monster Edwina!

Running after them, she confronted him outside the school.

"If you give me the antidote," she said, "I can fix everything!"

So he did!

Edwina and her gang were picking on Year seven pupils when Trina entered the canteen.

"Hey, Ed-weee-na!" she cried. "You're a fake! And I want you gone!"

The canteen watched as Trina faced her old victim.

"I challenge you to a fight!" she cried. "Winner takes all!"

CHAPTER 4
FIGHT!

And what a fight it was! Hair pulling, arm twisting, teeth baring, girls screaming.

Both girls were evenly matched – but Trina had the antidote!

And as Mandy, Candy and Sandy moved closer, yelling for Edwina to win...

She pulled it out!

The plan was to empty it on Edwina,
but a punch knocked it into the air.

It showered the antidote on all five girls!

As Edwina staggered back, Mandy, Candy
and Sandy started laughing. But then, all
five 'Mean Girls' started changing…

But that was a month ago.

Edwina's been back to normal since then, even getting Doctor Jekyll his job back. And she won the science competition last week!

Although it wasn't just her, she had help… from Trina, Mandy, Candy and Sandy… the 'Geeky Girls'!

STORY FACTS

Scientists are working on drugs that can make someone feel better about themselves.

Serotonin is a chemical in your brain that makes you feel good. Serotonin naturally increases on a sunny day – that's why sunny days can make you feel happier than rainy ones.

Scientists believe they can change our serotonin levels to boost our confidence. For example, more serotonin can't make you prettier, but it can make you **feel** prettier.

A little confidence can be a very good thing because it helps you believe in yourself. But too much confidence can make you rude and mean to others – just like in the story.

QUESTIONS

Who were the school bullies?
(page 6)

Where did Edwina spend her break times?
(page 8)

What happened to Doctor Jekyll?
(page 18)

Who got covered in the antidote?
(page 26)

What competition did Edwina and the other girls win?
(page 28)

Why do we feel better on a sunny day?
(page 30)

Writer, **Tony Lee**, was born in West London, UK in 1970. His books have been on the New York Bestseller list many times. He has also won the Eagle Award for writing comics.

Emmanuel Cerisier

I was born in France in 1970 and I live in Brittany with my family.

I studied graphic arts in Paris, then started to illustrate children's books. Now I also illustrate nonfiction, newspapers for children and covers for novels.